MALIQUE DEFEATS the BULLY

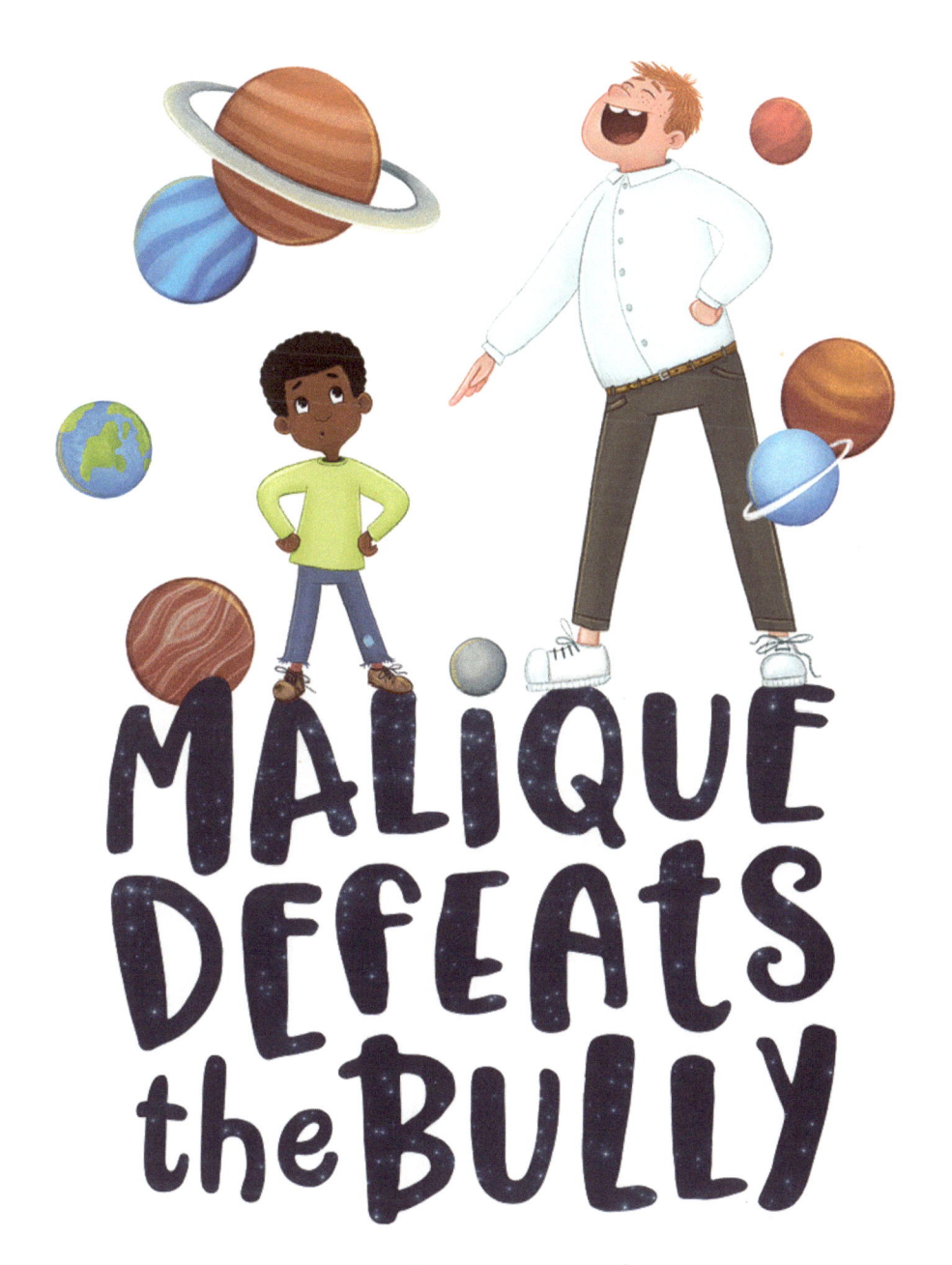

John Conde

illustrated by Elena Kochetova

Copyright © 2022 John Conde
All rights reserved
First Edition

Academic Function Motivations, LLC
Marietta, GA

First originally published by Academic Function Motivations 2022

ISBN 979-8-218-11353-7 (pbk)
ISBN 979-8-218-08483-7 (hc)
ISBN 979-8-218-11354-4 (digital)

Printed in the United States of America

There I was, sitting in seventh grade science class on a crisp fall day. Mr. Clyde, our science teacher, had just used his floor model of the solar system to help us visualize the revolution of the planets around the sun.

SATURN

MARS

VENUS

JUPITER

MERCURY

URANUS

EARTH

SUN

NEPTUNE

I exhaled in awe, fascinated by our solar system's gas giants, Neptune, Uranus, Saturn, and Jupiter.

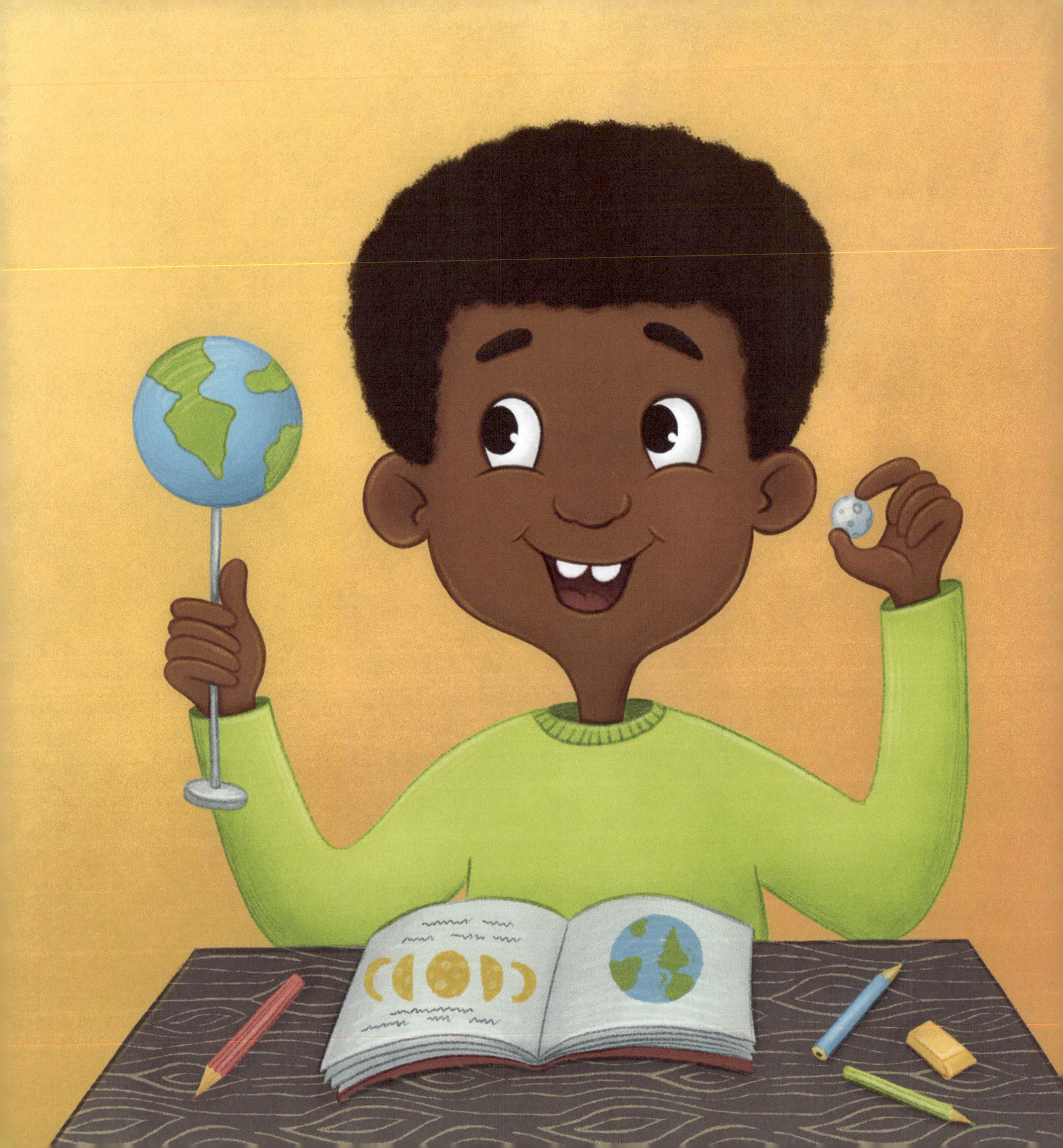

Our classroom overflowed with students from various backgrounds, most of who were eager to embrace the academic rigor that separates middle school from elementary. We had three Mikaylas, two Juans, three Andrews, but only one Malique — me. My small, square desk was located towards the front of the classroom, intentionally set apart from the few students who enjoyed being disobedient and not following the rules.

Mr. Clyde directed us to get into groups to collaborate on an assignment about the solar system. I was eager to get started with my group members, Rebeca and Johnny. Rebeca, a refugee student from Ukraine, had recently enrolled in our school after moving here due to the conflict in her country. She was a model student, always seated before the bell rang and the last to leave class.

And Johnny had just moved here from China. He communicated with us through an app that translated his native language to English.

As our group discussed the difference in temperature between the planets, Big Lee — he was called Big Lee because he was the same size as Mr. Clyde — stood up from his desk in the back corner of the classroom and proceeded to walk up to my desk while pointing at my faded jeans and slightly worn shoes. Without any provocation or remorse, he disrupted my group's exploration activity.

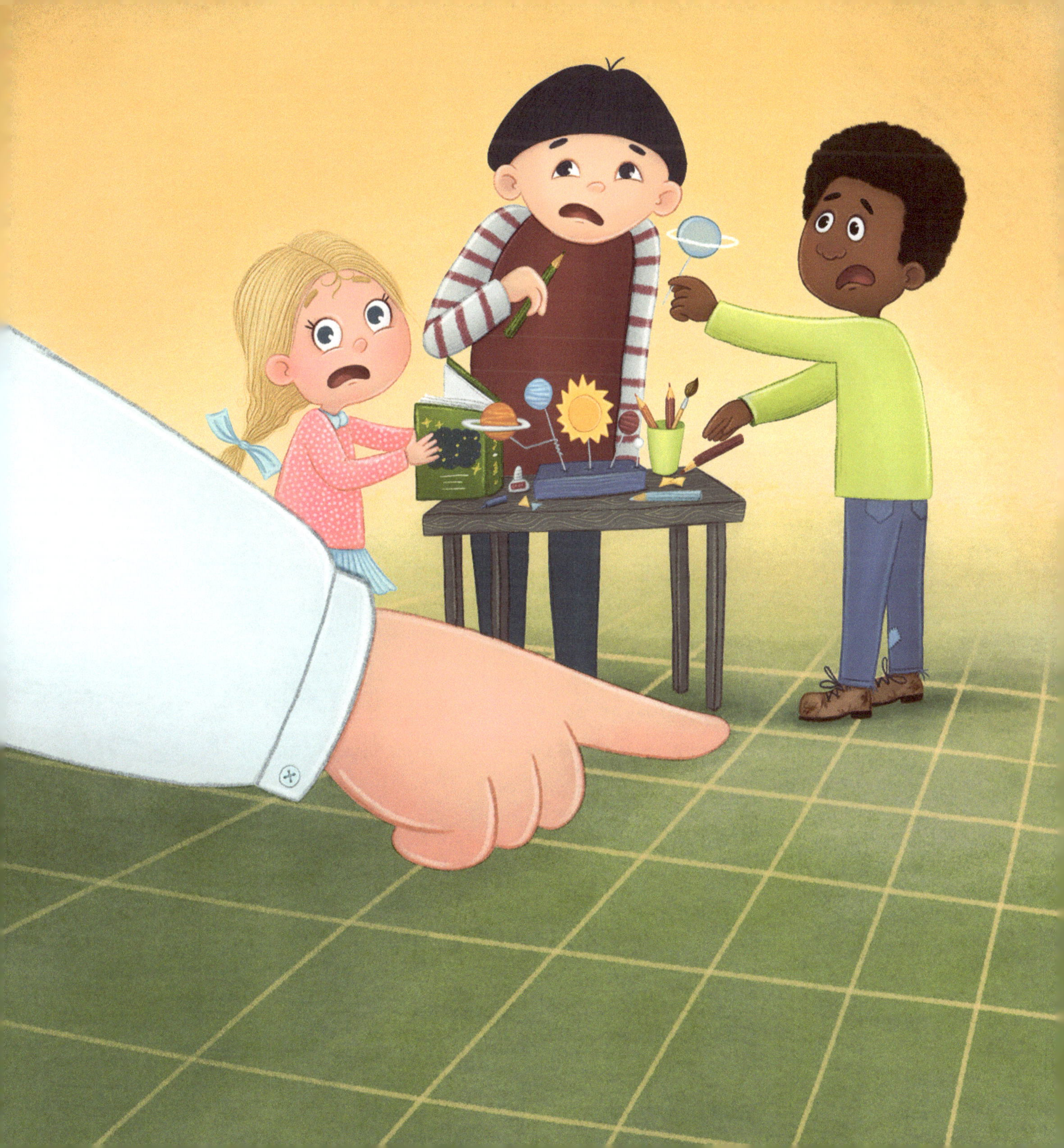

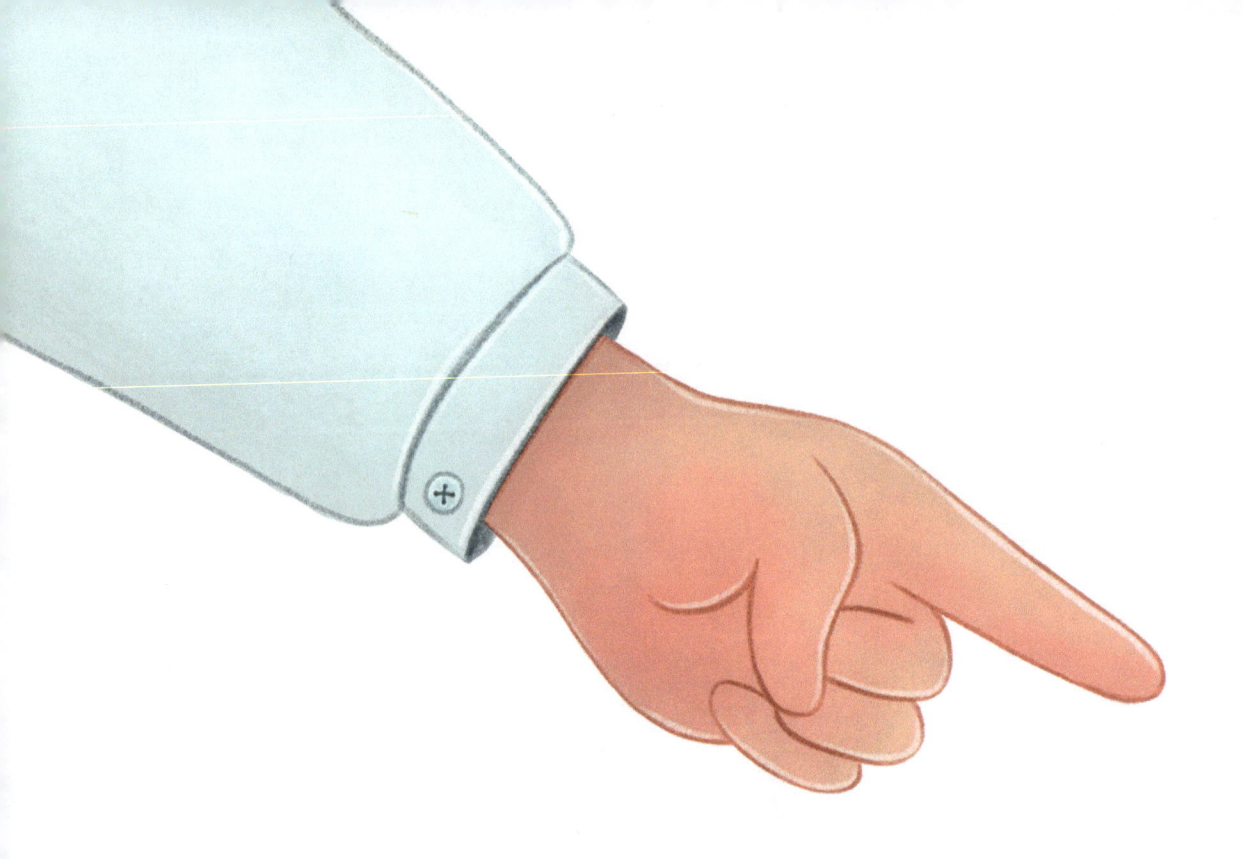

Big Lee pointed down at my jeans
that were frayed around the edges.

"Hey Malique! Those jeans are missing a tag in the back,"
he exclaimed.

"Where did you buy them from?
And your shoes look like you have had
them since the third grade!"

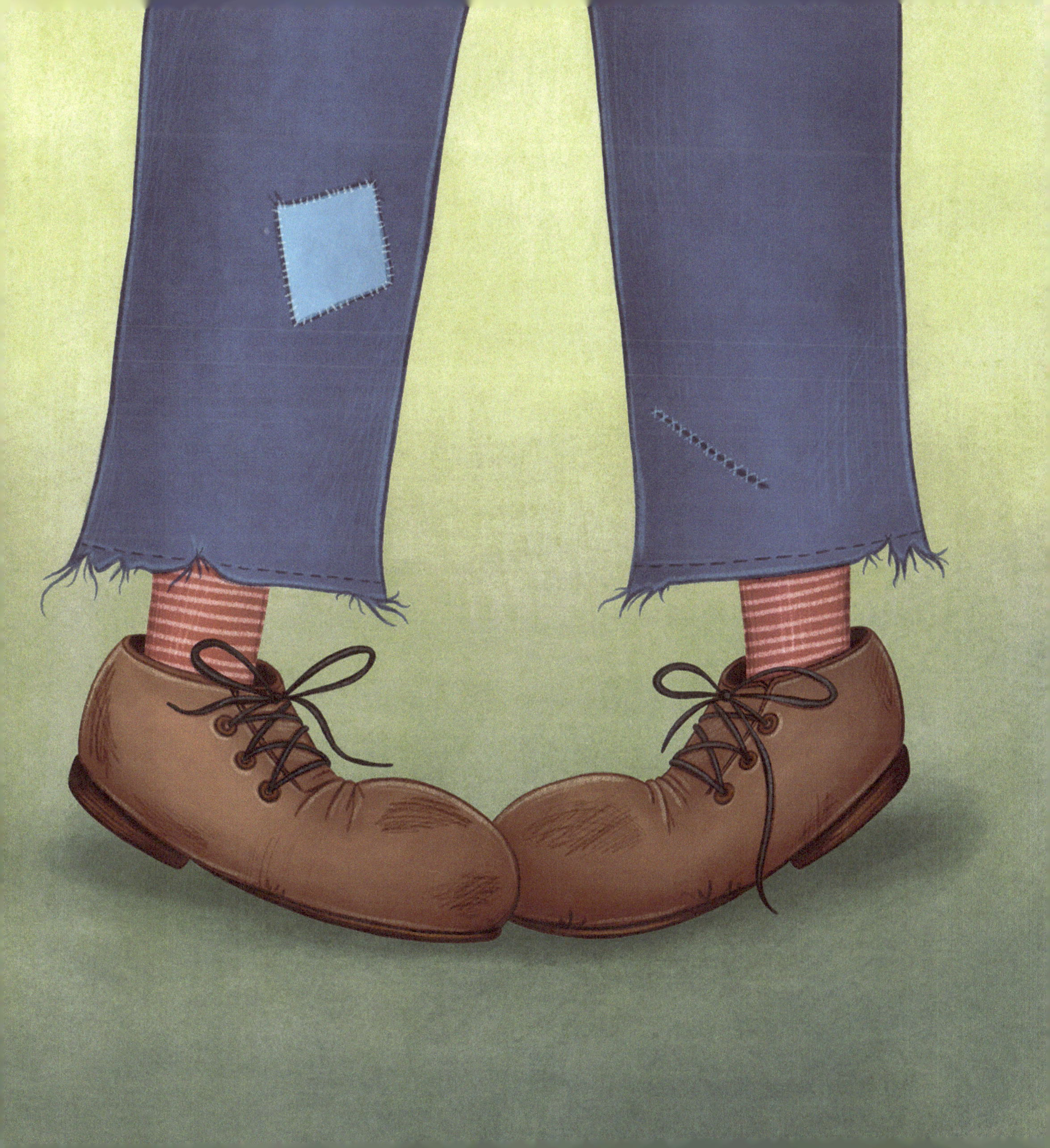

The class roared with laughter at Big Lee's rude comments, and he grinned widely, assuming he'd accomplished his goal of hurting my feelings.

However, Big Lee did not know I was prepared to be the victor of the unwanted war he'd just waged on my casual attire. Swiftly, I would end this spectacle quicker than he had started it.

Big Lee's bullying was intentional and intimidating. He stood tall and stuck his chest out, waiting for a response. His eyebrows contorted, and the tenseness in his face revealed his impatience for my response.

Silence fell across the classroom. Johnny placed his iPad on the table and looked up in shock. Rebeca's eyes peered over the top of a book she was reading as if she did not want anyone to see her looking.

VENUS (7,500 mi)
MARS (4,200 mi)
MERCURY (3,000 mi)
EARTH (7,900 mi)
SUN (865,000 mi)
JUPITER (89,000 mi)
SATURN (74,900 mi)
NEPTUNE (31,000 mi)
URANUS (32,000 mi)

Now, I refuse to agree, for even a second, with the myth that the price of material things like clothing determines the value of a person.

Big Lee's opinion about my choice of clothing was flawed, and I will never allow someone else's false ideology to influence my self-worth. Furthermore, I have always tried to interact with people using personality, humor, empathy, and kindness. I expect to be treated the same way by others.

Big Lee appeared smug as he challenged me to a response simply with the look on his face. I was emotionally calm, thinking about the best response. Like forming a hypothesis in science, using facts based on observations, I considered my word choices.

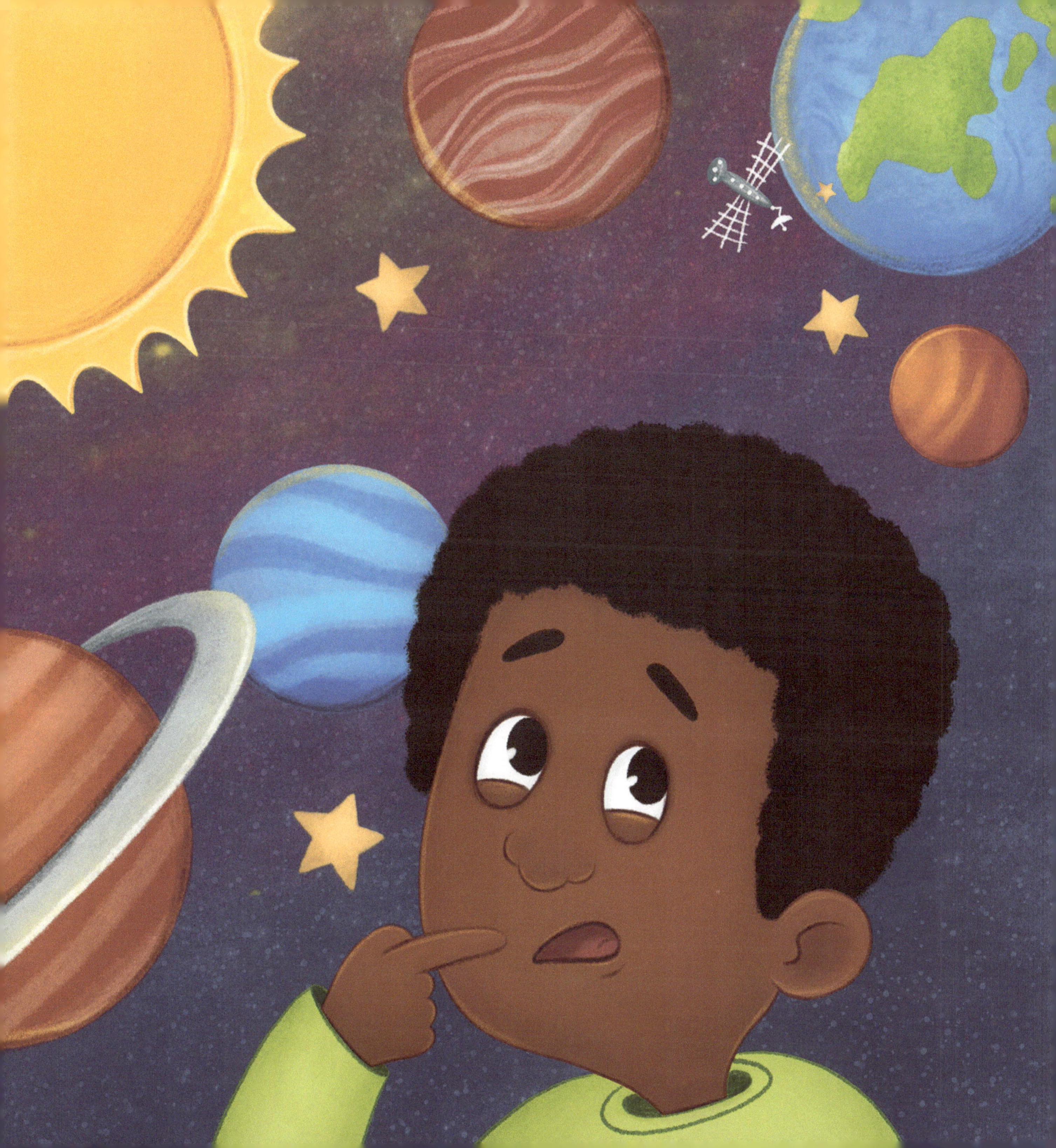

Finally, I had the perfect answer for Big Lee! With all the eyes in the completely silent classroom on me, I glanced at Lee's pristine white tennis shoes and freshly ironed collared shirt. And then I confidently asked,

"how is that working for you?"

How is that working for you?

Big Lee looked stunned. He blinked a few times, and his lips moved like he was going to say something. But then he just walked away with a confused look on his face.

Big Lee learned a valuable lesson that day — that words used to describe you should never be used to define you.

I was not about to allow his problem to become my problem. In the end, Lee realized I was just as confident in my slightly worn shoes and frayed jeans as he was in his pressed, collared shirt and new tennis shoes.

Rebeca resumed reading her book while smiling with relief, the class whispered to one another in disbelief, and we all returned to what was most important in middle school — obtaining a quality education!

After school that day, Johnny told me, "Malique, I am no longer going to worry about someone teasing me about my communication app. From now on, I'll just say, 'how's that working for you?'"

How is that working for you?

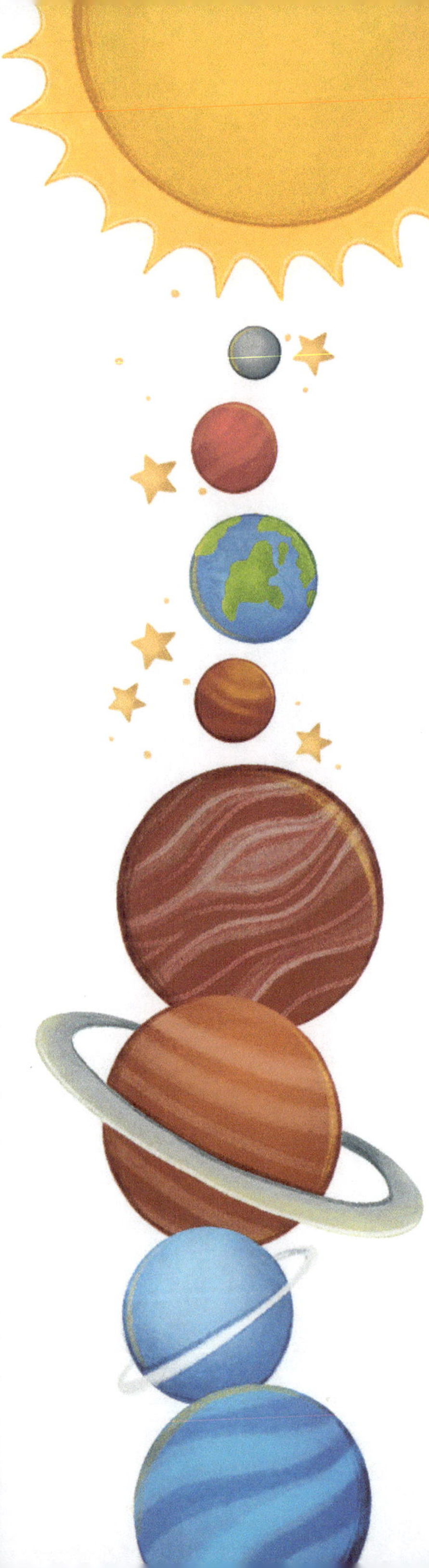

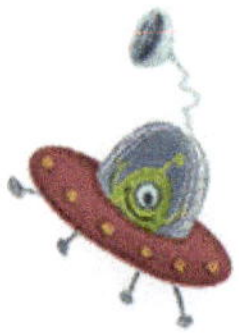

John Conde lives with his wife and two sons in Georgia, where he enjoys traveling, playing the guitar, cooking, and participating in Boy Scouts activities with his children. He was inspired to write "Malique Defeats the Bully" by interacting with his colleagues and the youth in the community. John uses engaging storytelling to demonstrate the importance of setting goals, regulating emotions, and changing behavior.